HISTORIES OF MEMORIES

Fort Smith, Arkansas

Praise for *Histories of Memories*:

"In the vulnerable, gorgeously written, and brilliantly illustrated *Histories of Memories*, Shome Dasgupta offers the reader an unflinching account of love and loss, failure and redemption, pleasure and pain. Dasgupta layers locations—Kolkata, Edmonton, Munich—with soundtracks—*Dr. Dolittle*, *The Perks of Being a Wallflower*, *Magnolia*—and family—mother, father, uncle, brother, with friends, lifelong and long gone: a mixtape filled with his distinctive lyricism. On this carefully curated journey, where he sometimes takes our hands, leading us along winding paths, and other times flings us far out into space or drops us deep into a swirl of firing synapses, Dasgupta is always pushing us and himself to uncover, discover, recover meaning and, ultimately, memory."

—Melissa Llanes Brownlee, author of *Hard Skin* and *Kahi and Lua*

"Memories can coax and soothe. They can break us in an instant or help to heal deep wounds. It makes no difference if they are whole or fragmented; memories pull us around in time, whether we're prepared for that journey or not, and bring us straight back into the sounds and tastes and feelings and dreams that make us who we are. That's exactly the force harnessed by Shome Dasgupta's new collection of stories, *Histories of Memories*. Page by page, these stories transport, restore, nourish, and remind. They bring us chocolates and curries, mud and family, songs and sights from all over the planet. More than anything, they show us humanity. And for that, for this author, I am truly grateful."

—Jack B. Bedell, author of *Against the Woods' Dark Trunks*, Poet Laureate of Louisiana, 2017–2019

"Shome Dasgupta charts a sometimes surreal and always beautiful crossing of time and space. From a dead cow on the side of a dirt road to the infinite cosmos of space, *Histories of Memories* spirals through tales of joy, loss, and grief, suggesting that loss is not an end. The past is always accessible, even as it shapeshifts on the altars of remembrance. Dasgupta reveals the radiant potentials of short form storytelling. His stories and sketches operate with their own internal logic, their own form and pacing. Each is its own testament to the memory monuments created by a dream, a song on the radio, a favorite childhood book, or a sip of Indian cola. In this collection, nothing settles. Every page is a new arrival that opens a door to a new destination already changing, and every new entryway is exactly where you want to be."

—Ra'Niqua Lee, author of *For What Ails You*

Praise for *The Muu-Antiques*:

"A new book by Shome Dasgupta is always a cause for celebration, and *The Muu-Antiques* is brilliant, off-kilter in the best ways, and it's a wise, beautiful, and surprising novel. It is such a wonderful addition to his body of work."

—Rob Roberge, Author of *Liar* and *The Cost of Living*

"It's rare to find a book that has you rooting for both friend and foe, and then have both stick with you long after you turn the last page. This is Dasgupta's greatest gift: find the good in everyone and let that be remembered long afterwards, like a fine antique."

—Toby LeBlanc, Author of *Dark Roux*

Praise for *Tentacles Numbing*:

"Shome Dasgupta makes a unique and important contribution to diverse diasporic South Asian literature and we are lucky to have this book."

—Chaya Bhuvaneswar, author of *White Dancing Elephants*

"With sharp prose and disarming vulnerability, Shome Dasgupta offers a sensitive novel about grief, human connection, and holding onto reasons to live—even when they sting."

—Anuja Varghese, author of *Chrysalis*

Praise for *Cirrus Stratus*:

"The only thing stopping Shome Dasgupta is his imagination, which knows no bounds."

—Sara Lippmann, author of *Lech*

HISTORIES OF MEMORIES

SHOME DASGUPTA

Histories of Memories

Cover image:
Tortoise shell photo by Joshua J. Cotten (via Unsplash)
Stained glass via Canva

Edited by Casie Dodd
Design & typography by Belle Point Press

Belle Point Press, LLC
Fort Smith, Arkansas
bellepointpress.com
editor@bellepointpress.com

Find Belle Point Press
on Facebook,
Twitter (@BellePointPress),
and Instagram (@bellepointpress)

Printed in the United States of America

27 26 25 24 23 1 2 3 4 5

Library of Congress Control Number: 2023946413

ISBN: 978-1-960215-08-6

HOM/BPP18

For
Chad & Bianca

Contents

Like Hummingbirds

LIKE WHEN we sat on the sun and watched the world simmer in our heads, brother—remember that time? And how you were so furious and the words from your mouth smoldered, drifting toward every star, making sure there was no void. The pain. The pain you felt became ashes in my own body, and I'm so sorry, brother. I was helpless. And as much as I felt your pain, there was nothing I could do to take it away from you. Your skull vibrated as the smoke left through every pore of your body, and I just wanted to hold you, even if it meant I'd burn, but you wouldn't let me. You knew. You recognized, despite all that was happening, that you loved me and didn't want to hurt me. Remember in that brief gleam of light, before you or I left, how the sun diminished and we floated in space no longer knowing if the world existed or cared if it did or not, and we hovered around like the hummingbirds in our back yard, trying not to bump into stars. We had so much fun and for that endless second you found peace as you took my hand and guided me around, much like you did in life. You loved those hummingbirds.

Brother, I fucked up so much. I'm so sorry.

And like before it all happened, when you were there we would be on our hands and knees, crawling in the ditch, pretending to be raccoons because there were no more raccoons left to feed. They went away just like you or me. But when we were playing, I cut my leg and cried so loud. You picked me up to take me home but I flailed so much we tumbled over, and the world was before us as we were on our backs. My pain went away as we tried to count all the birds in the sky.

And brother, I don't know—I don't know if I had the chance to do it all over again if I would change any of it. Including all the times I fucked up and all the times you had to pull on my arm while I was sinking. I don't know if I would change it all up because look at who we became—I honestly think our parents would be so proud of us. How we made it through even though we weren't meant to—I know who we are now, but if I could go back and change all the ways I needed to change, I don't know who we would become.

You'd be so proud of me now, brother. I'm sorry. I'm glad you no longer feel any pain. I feel it every now and then, but then it all goes away when it's just us, floating around in space, drifting this way and that, toward every star, and every now and then a hummingbird appears, glowing and holy, fluttering its wings to let us know that we're here. How you loved those hummingbirds, brother, I will never forget—even with closed eyes, I will never forget.

And this might be the last time we can speak—I don't know if you can hear me—I'm not sure how all of this goes, but I love you, brother. Thanks for always being there.

Chapel of Ghosts

A BLANK DAY it was, the day we threw broken pieces of road at the blue and green stained-glass windows. We were nowhere and that's all we knew—being nowhere and doing nothing until nothing got us in trouble. The sun was fresh out from the horizon, and we hadn't slept yet—walking along dew-ridden fields in the middle of the night was what made us sane—it was the only time we felt like we existed—when nothing was around, and it was just us and croaking frogs, walking in unknown lands.

The stained-glass windows were already in shards by the time we found the chapel, made of rotting wood and covered in messy vines, twirling in every direction as if they were searching for the meaning of their existence. We just made the broken windows more broken. There was no roof.

She pointed to the door that was on the ground, covered in dirt, crumbling and looking sad. The entrance was there—waiting for us—and we walked in holding hands, leaving the morning fog behind us. Refracted light came through the teething windows, revealing crunched pews and a sliced altar. It was pure demolition and desolation and we were happy. She threw her last piece of road at one of the windows, and with her other hand guided me up to the front of the chapel where we knelt in broken glass and wood. And so we prayed.

And we prayed until our holy thoughts drifted toward the sound of footsteps coming from the entrance. We stood up and realized that there was no way really out except for the way we came in. There they were—two of them—or the two of us—our own ghosts in different forms of our own memories. Bruised—smiling—bloodied—crying—sleeping—laughing—beaten—holding hands. Our past before us as the entrance way to the chapel shifted backgrounds for each memory. And there we were—in her grandfather's attic, she covered in blood, me, holding a pipe—listening to the sound of his footsteps. And there we were, in uncut fields, running through, feeling nothing because nothing was all we ever wanted. In the pond, underwater, holding each other as we counted the bubbles from our breath. In cuffs, expressing our love for each other as the moon shone on the gloss of her eyes. And there we were—in the woods, looking for bear prints and red petals.

We held hands and watched ourselves—her body trembled, my body trembled, we trembled, our cries became louder with each memory, our hands clasping tighter, until our legs gave in and we fell. *No more, no more, no more*, she said, banging her head against wood and dirt. *More, more, more*, she said, banging her hands against the wood and dirt. *Let us go*, she said, our tears dampening the land around us in streams and drips. The voices stopped. The silence began, and we were there inside of it. How many broken bones of love and sadness, we didn't know. We never counted.

There went our memories—all gone, our backs on the broken chapel floor. We were inside of silence. We were nowhere again and happy. Our bruises, our scars, swept away in a dream, no longer to return. She said it was time to go and so we did, leaving the caved chapel, our tower of light, holding hands and never looking back.

Between the Bars

The Learning Game

THE COW lay dead in the middle of the road. Jack pointed at it.

"Cat," he said.

"That's not a cat," Ray said. "That's a cow. That's a dead cow, Jack."

We were once happy.

"Pull over," Ray said. "There's no one behind us. There's no one anywhere. We're all alone, in the middle of nothing, with this dead cow on a dumb road. I want to take a break."

Break? I've been driving for five hours.

I went to the side of the dirt road, which looked endless in the wavering air full of mirages. The only thing else around us were bales of hay in the distance. As soon as we got out of the car, we started to sweat.

"Damn," Ray said.

"Damn," Jack said.

"No," Ray replied. "You can't say that word. Only adults can say that word. Adults, Jack, not you."

"Damn," Jack said again.

Ray raised his voice: "Stop. Stop."

We were all already drenched in sweat.

"Let it go," I said. "He doesn't know any better or what it means. He's just repeating, learning."

I took Jack by the hand, and we walked toward the cow. I loved the way he wobbled from side to side, still trying to make sense of his own body and the world around him. Despite the heat and the carcass, and Ray, it was a pleasurable moment, walking side by side, hand in hand with the little one.

"It must have just died," I said. "There isn't a stench. Poor thing."

"It's a cow," Ray said. "We just ate some hamburgers yesterday. Who cares."

I ran my hand through Jack's fledgling hair, damp and soft. He was looking around, observing all that he could, taking it all in. To us, we were nowhere—to him, we were everywhere. I picked Jack up and propped him against my body and breathed in his hair.

"You're being mean," I said.

I wasn't expecting an apology.

"It's a cow."

I waited for it.

"Damn."

"Damn," Jack said.

Ray threw his arms in the air and walked in circles for a few seconds like a dog. Jack pointed at the dead cow.

"Cat," he said.

"Cow," Ray said. "That's a dead cow, Jack."

I gave up and didn't bother saying anything. I had already given up years ago, before we even adopted Jack. Five years ago to be exact. Right now, I was only in it for Jack, coming up with plans to get out of it—just me and Jack. No Ray. It'll happen.

"Hey Jack," I said. "Look—that's a cow."

I whispered into his ear.

"Meow meow," Jack replied.

Ray didn't hear him. He was too busy thinking about himself. How did this happen? Why was I still with him? I couldn't help but to remember when we were first in love. And then it all changed—his mood, his temper. He was just unhappy all the time. A jerk. And it became worse when we started to take care of Jack. Good memories only elongate the bad ones.

"Cat!" Jack shouted. "Cat! Cat! Cat!"

He continued to point at the dead cow.

"No," Ray said. "No. Stop it. You should know this by now. That's a cow. It goes moo. It's a damn cow, Jack. We ate one yesterday."

I heard him whisper "idiot" to himself.

I looked down the road, and in the distance, I saw a car heading this way. Good enough. At least he won't be stranded. Or maybe he will. I held Jack tightly, pressing him against my body, and headed toward the car as Ray was looking the other way, standing at the feet of the dead cow. Trying to be as gentle as possible, I sat Jack down in the back seat, buckled him up, and got into the driver's side. As I turned the ignition on, Ray turned around.

"What are you doing?"

What am I doing?

"Hey. Hey. What are you doing?"

I eased the car up and put the window down.

"I hope you're happy. I hope you'll be happy. It's just you and the dead cow."

"What the fuck are you doing? Fuck."

I sped off, barely missing the cow. I looked at Ray in the rearview mirror, standing there with his arms in the air.

"Fuck," Jack said.

And I laughed—it was a loud, good laugh, one I hadn't felt in years.

Listen to Track #10

Aaliyah

Dr. Dolittle Soundtrack
Track #3

Damn. This was the song—the song we danced to in perfect rhythm with each other. No words—just movement, and it was all in our shoulders. I never saw the movie, but I got the soundtrack for that one song, and every time I think about that song, I think about how we danced and they watched.

I remember once, when I was picking her up, on a rainy night, to go watch *Rounders*, and I had *One In A Million* playing on cassette in the Buick. Years later, after we went our different ways, she still remembered her—she still remembered us.

"Aaliyah is playing on the stereo right now" was all the message said, and it was all I ever needed to read. She remembered.

OutKast

Aquemini
Track #10

We were driving around once—I played this song on repeat. Most specifically, just the opening part, over and over again.

And she laughed, and every time it's storming outside, I think about that drive.

Aimee Mann

Magnolia Soundtrack
Track #1

This movie was full of magic, and when "One" started playing during the movie, she mentioned how she loved this song. Later I bought the soundtrack and listened to this song, just this song—I'm not sure what else was on that album, it was only this song.

That scene with all the frogs—it's hard not to think about her when I think about frogs.

Elliott Smith

Good Will Hunting Soundtrack
Track #1

First off, I didn't know coffee or how to drink it or any of the other espresso drinks. We went to the bookstore café before going to the movie theater. She knew what to order, and I didn't, and I didn't even know how to order so I just quickly asked for an Americano, pretending that I knew what I was doing. Every question the barista asked, I responded with saying yes so confidently. We sat down and I took a sip and wanted to spit it all out, trying hard not to cough—when she left to use the restroom, I poured all of it out into the bin, leaving only a sip or two in the cup. And when she got back, I finished off my drink and mentioned that we should head over to the theater.

I honestly didn't know that Elliott Smith would be on the soundtrack. I had no clue. And when this song started playing—damn. Too many emotions to understand but all that I knew was that I was there, with her, and Elliott Smith was playing.

Elliott Smith

Good Will Hunting Soundtrack
Track #9

I don't think there was much else to say.

Spice Girls

Spice
Track #1

We were driving to a track meet in your Wrangler, which was about an hour away. We got lost, and we were late for the meet, but we didn't miss any of our events. It was a pretty day—sunny. I had to hold the starting block for the 200m she was about to run. She said she was so nervous, and I tried to tell her a knock, knock joke.

"Not now," she said and laughed.

And the horn went off and she ran.

But she laughed.

Pulp

Great Expectations Soundtrack
Track #6

When Finn starts to sketch Estella, and as the song eventually gets faster—the feeling of raw love, this strange thrill of seeing and hearing and experiencing art and art and art all combined into a crazy energy of confusion and chaos. I remember I wanted to turn my head to her. But I couldn't—so nervous, so lost.

And then of course, later on:

"Don't you understand that everything I do, I do it for you? Anything that might be special in me, is you."

Damn.

Radiohead

The Bends
Track #10

I'm guessing she knew it was me who put this in her car while she was away. I should have put the track number to listen to, though—there was that one line, that one line that made me think about her every time I heard it. I listened to that one line on repeat—constantly pressing the back button on my Discman, just for that one part.

That one song—that line, when I was in India during the winter break, that was all I played. In the Kolkata traffic, at the flat, walking around, restaurants, everywhere—the rest of the world just faded away.

Cracker

The Perks Of Being A Wallflower Soundtrack
Track #7

This was the last movie we watched together in the movie theater—some ten plus years later. When this song came on—I felt just as I did way back when, sitting next to you, nervous and shy, emotional. I was sixteen all over again. And that ending—damn, that ending, it got to me and got to me like I was in love fifteen years ago in an alternate universe. I don't know if we'll be able to watch another movie again, together at the theater, but if we don't—I wouldn't have it any other way, for this to be the last movie. It will certainly last in infinity.

Angeles
sun
So nice to meet you
Hi, I'm Angeles
Say Yes
(the morning after)

Upon a Sunny Day at Noon

She (they thought that she was floating—a universe in herself, encompassing the magic of the unknown and no one dared to ask her, talk to her, look at her as she emitted an aura of such wonderful power, there was nothing but silence, and in that silence, the world was rotating in such a magnitude, that the earth shook a bit, causing the seismologists, who were just getting ready to eat lunch, to glance at their machines) watched the storm approach while holding an avocado in her left hand.

Musica Universalis and the Pythagorean Love Song

Theorem as it was as bale and bale across a dew-singed plain settled in silence, and so side by side they went in a pair to search for conjectures of breadth—only to split at angle's base like raised arms in plea to close their eyes and feel their ankles traced against pressed meadow and straw, they knew not if they were to meet again. A chance they took, no longer adjacent or faced—vertices diminished, famished and worn they strayed from tangent and vertex to find themselves in opposite planes. Tilted like this and that, no echo to be heard or a whisper to grasp in hand's reach—buried in coat of night they thought of all the ways they never spoke. Gentle vibrations of wings and murmurs to keep them company, alone they as they were—no sine or sign of any line or degree to climb to shout for their care and well being. Let star and star and moon and rock enter in on pastured graze, they slept on roots and tufts for heat and health—away their dreams adrift and coast and all along in space and system, comet and comet their thoughts met and greeted on cusp and corner. Such a journey astray it was thought only to be known that all along their side and length were never divided regardless of distance and measure—their heads were mazed and tunneled in ghostly shadow in crest and rift. Would they meet again on soft-patched earth and sewn and quilt they didn't question—and for together they'll be in migration of eternities no matter the case—in dreams they delivered and declared all the words they never grasped before. Let them sleep and rest on Pythagorean tunes—let orb and sun let sing their symphonies in rotation's hum as then and for now and forever let be, entombed and enlightened. Shone affinity beyond any degree of calculation, there was no death but mere reckonings of elements and axioms, replicated and renewed.

Excerpts from My Memory

Vienna, Austria, 1988
There was bread—my dad was being chased by ducks.

Edmonton, Alberta, 1990
My place of birth, and this was the first time I visited after moving away when I was just one. At the mall, there was a car store, and there was also a water park—I ate a pretzel.

Munich, Germany, 1988
My only friend was named Bastian—we couldn't understand each other so we just raced down the street each evening. I never won, and he punched me one time.

Singapore, 1987
At the Changi Airport, my parents bought my brother the first Guns N' Roses album, *Appetite For Destruction*—on cassette. I wasn't allowed to listen to it, but I turned the skull with the top hat from the cover art into a superhero in my stick-figure drawings.

Kolkata, India 1999

We were standing outside Flurys, a confectionary and tearoom, waiting for it to open. There was a huge crowd, and people started to push each other, trying to get to the front of the vanishing line. My dad was pushed, and I started to shout, telling everyone to stop. They all just stared at me—not sure if they understood me or cared or both, but after a few seconds, they started nudging each other again. At this time, they didn't have Coca-Cola or Pepsi, but a brand known as Thums Up.

Vancouver, British Columbia, 1990

My brother's birthplace, and my first visit—we were with our relatives, and I watched *Dead Poets Society* for the first time, and it was the first time a movie made me cry.

Kolkata, India, 2003

There was Coca-Cola. My grandfather no longer used his typewriter—he stayed in bed for most of the time. His library was my imagination, and I started using his typewriter just so he could remember the sounds of his own imagination.

Manchester, England, 1993

Parrs Wood High School—my fellow classmate crushed a Sunkist can on my head and pushed me back. It was a pretty day.

KOLKATA, INDIA, 1999

My grandmother, on my mother's side, was deep into Parkinson's disease. She would put her palm on my face—it shook, but it was full of our past memories.

ATHENS, GREECE, 1992

At the hotel where we were staying, late at night in the lobby, we watched the Dream Team play in the Olympics in black and white. Sometimes we couldn't watch because someone else was watching soap operas—the goal was to get to the lobby before him. I also learned how to play chess.

KOLKATA, INDIA, 1994

At the Ramakrishna Mission Institute of Culture, where my brother, dad, and I stayed—we ate toast and eggs every morning, and late at night, we watched soccer in black and white at an outdoor commons area on a semi-broken TV. I also read *Jurassic Park* and *The Lord Of The Rings* trilogy. We buried our grandmother on my father's side.

MUNICH, GERMANY, 1988

On TV, at our flat, I watched for the first time the music video for Tiffany's "I Think We're Alone Now." It made me want to go to a mall, and I remember falling in love.

Kolkata, India, 2003

They had a new donut store, and a mall that sold jeans. I miss the cows who controlled traffic rather than the traffic lights. I miss the scent of sizzling fish mixed in with freshly handwashed clothes hung out to dry on the balcony, right next to a bucket of marigolds. I miss my grandparents.

Paris, France, 1992

The Bulls were losing to the Knicks, and it was the first time I saw the works of Picasso, as we visited The Musée Picasso.

Kolkata, India, 1999

This was the last time I saw my grandmother.

Kolkata, India, 2003

This was the last time I saw my grandfather.

Lafayette, Louisiana, 2020

I was in my room, time traveling, thinking about how the past has all led to this moment. And now, all I can see are marigolds.

Golden Fields

I WAS FIVE years old at the time—this was in 1986, when we lived in our first house in Lafayette, LA. Our neighborhood, Fox Chase, was a quiet and friendly one, and the street we lived on, Golden Fields, was full of driveways with basketball goals, and this was where I spent an endless number of hours shooting hoops, hoping that the basketball would reach the rim or backboard or anything but air. I'm short now and, of course, was much shorter then, and I had to use my utmost amount of energy to push the ball toward the goal.

I had a couple of neighborhood friends back then—some were my age and some were a bit older. My closest friend was on the other side of our house. We spent countless hours playing basketball or pretending to be Transformers, He-Man, or G.I Joe characters. I had another friend who lived in the same subdivision but not on the same street—I didn't know that he was white and I didn't know that I was brown then. His name was C______, and we were pretty good at falling off of our bikes. One evening, just before the sun was going down, C______ and I were playing in the front yard of his house, searching for four-leaf clovers. I had just found one, when C______ asked me if I was a ______. I had never heard of the word, and I wasn't sure, so all I could answer was that I didn't know. It was just about to get dark so I had to run back home to wash up before getting dinner, watching *Looney Tunes*, and going to bed.

I was in the bathtub—my mother was washing me. As she poured water over me to clear off the soap, I looked at her and asked her if I was a ______. I remember her eyes narrowing; she stopped pouring the water over my head and though I still had a bit of soap in my eyes, I could see that my mom looked angry—angry like when I had done something wrong or when I was in trouble. She asked me where I had heard that word. I told her. She told me to never say that word again, without any explanation as to why other than that it was a bad word. Her anger turned to sadness, and it looked like she was about to cry. She poured water over me one more time before telling me to dry up.

Since that evening—of searching for four-leaf clovers in his yard and hearing the word ______ for the first time and asking my mom about it, my mom told me that I couldn't play with C______ anymore. And I didn't. And I didn't know why, but to see that pain and anger in my mother's eyes, that was all it took. I just continued to shoot hoops with my neighbors or play He-Man or Transformers. I still didn't know if I was a ______, but my wonder vanished after getting stung by a bee for the first time in the front yard of my house. And to be honest, 35-odd years later, I still don't know if I am or not.

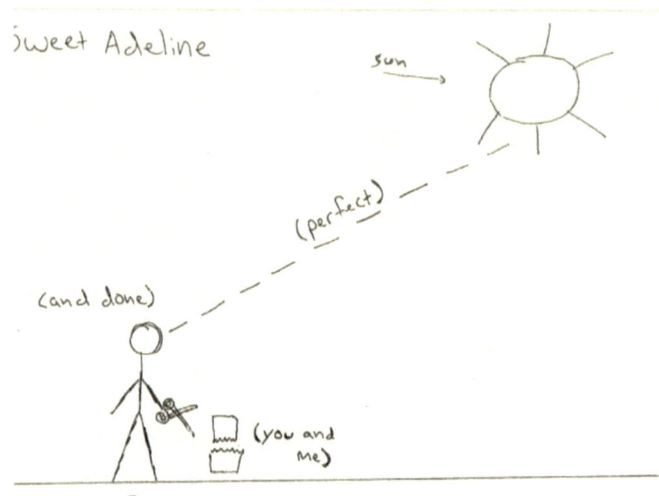

Baby Britain

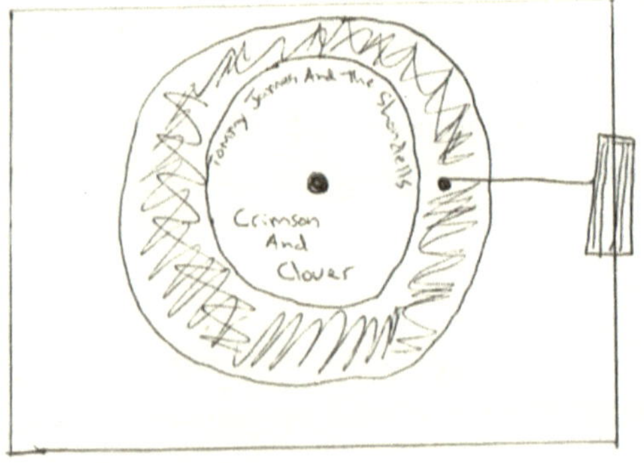

Sound of Dew

And it's in this confusion, this silent internal chaos of confliction, where it yearns to thrive and live and pulsate, scornfully or sorrowfully, perhaps feeling guilty about its own doing. It's a blemished line—or hazed, distorted mirrors where there's no clear image, being sorry to be here or there or anywhere but nowhere and somewhere in there, a thought of joy.

I once saw a dead squirrel on the road—I was on my way to get my morning coffee, or iced mocha, rather—I just made a turn and there it lay. It was a pretty morning, one that felt like fresh dew grazing your ankles, and it wasn't so much the dead squirrel that made me sad but there was this other squirrel, which stood on its hind legs for just a second and then it took two hops before passing the dead squirrel—such glee in motion.

Like sediments buried in the horizon, knowing that if there ever is a breath, that the chest oscillates with apprehension because the mind is aware what is waiting for it, incessantly. I don't know—there's a constant search for solace, such sadness in wires dropped about and tangled, draped against bone and cartilage.

The squirrel looked so happy or cheerful—the one that was alive—and it went about its way, perhaps in search of nourishment or to climb a tree to jump from branch to branch, making the leaves frolic to and fro—a rustling under a sun which had just made its bed. And the other was dead, always—its puffed tail—arched, one last memory.

Haphazard—haphazard fickle sunbeam, feign such sprinkle, such and so squint eyes under a sound of dew where leaf and leaf envelop a knoll of lost time. An axe, in its gleam so heavy under illuminated creations—wearing two sides of mashing sensations. A mirror and a mirror—a curtain strewn about a skull full of rattling pebbles, an arbor and infinite hallway.

I saw a turtle—this wasn't long ago, after the age of dead squirrels and light. So again it was morning—taking a turn, there on the side with its head gallant and calm as ever, trying to make it over there. A pond was on the other side—the other side. I couldn't stop—there was too much around. I couldn't stop to lift this shell and help it across the way. There was too much around. That was what I told myself.

"Yes, please—I would like a medium iced mocha."

Knock knock knock—how it would sound, a tap on a home—soporific, like a lullaby from eons ago in which an echo rippled gently into a mouth of river. Rivers—entwine, entangle, encompass—a grasp for a hand or a tongue or a reflection. Taunting dichotomies—magic of other kinds where a world and a wand disappear amid a quake caused by a song made of wishing wells.

"Oh that would be it—thank you."

And at the drive-thru, as I waited—I don't know for how long—it felt like forever as I thought about the turtle and if it made it over. Over there. I didn't return home until the evening, sun half-asleep in a lazy wind, and I stopped just at that point where the turtle was crossing and I backed up just a bit to let the beams shine on the asphalt, and there was nothing—no remnants, no cracked bits, no vague mound, no unrecognizable creation. There was nothing. And as I made it home, I thought about how I'll go back again at dawn just to check again. And as I made it home, I thought about how I'm afraid of certain mornings.

$1000 to Lose

I BECOME SAD whenever I watch *Wheel Of Fortune*. Just the other day it happened again—I was watching an episode at the hotel, and two of the contestants were winning a good bit of money, but the third person, Lena—I believe was her name—just couldn't accrue any cash. She was kind. A mother of two, her husband was a veteran and she herself was a hairstylist. Curly brown hair, most likely dyed, with little cosmetics, dressed in a bright flowery blouse. She never rushed to spin the wheel and she didn't interrupt Pat Sajak, always patient and waiting her turn, almost like she counted to three before reaching over and grabbing a spoke—almost like she had a life full of many challenges and didn't take any experience for granted.

I hope the kids are doing okay at home. This is the first time I've left them since they were born. I'm glad to have a good friend in Bay to watch them. I'll need to get her a gift as a thank you for taking them in for these few days.

When Lena was able to spin the wheel, she would get a letter every now and then, but then she would lose it all after landing on bankrupt. Or she would lose a turn, and the person after her would spin just once before solving the puzzle. Lena would genuinely smile and clap as the others won. I had never seen someone so happy about losing to others, especially when it came to money. I can't remember too much about the other two contestants other than that I didn't like them. One was a man and the other was a woman, and they just came off as mean, pushy, and their personalities matched their physical looks. There are always the other two.

I hope the kids don't tear their school clothes or dirty them too much. I'm a bit low on money this month, but hopefully it'll change soon. It's important to remain positive—got to. For my kids' sake—I can't show them any other way. I wish Mom was still alive.

And at the end, when it was all over, Lena shook everyone's hand and gave Pat a hug after not winning anything. She had this gleam in her eye like she just saw the most amazing magic trick. And it wasn't just that episode—it's like there's always one person in every *Wheel Of Fortune* who is like Lena. Just happy and sweet no matter what. I wish. They did give Lena $1000, but that probably went to all of the travel and hotel costs as she came all the way from Maine.

$1000. I could do wonders with that right now—more than anything else, I just want to take my kids out for a nice dinner and maybe even a movie after. It would be nice to lose.

I hope Lena is doing okay. I hope they are all doing okay, the ones who never win but are always smiling sunbeams. I need to send the sanitation workers a thank you note—it has been awhile since I've thanked them. I hope the kids are having fun.

Oh, is he talking to me? Focus. Yes, he's talking to me. Here we go.

Yes, Pat—I'm ready—thank you! Yes, Pat, sorry, I was in a

daze—this is all so amazing!

1-2-3.

It's quite a stretch to reach over and grab the wheel—I have to suck in my stomach a bit. Here we go. When it stops, I'll go with L.

I hope the kids are doing okay.

A Vague Recollection from 111 Liberty Avenue

My first night in rehab, I was put in a room with a heroin addict. I was groggy from the medicine the nurse had given me to soften the cut from alcohol—for an alcoholic, or for any kind of addict for that matter, immediately quitting could cause some internal issues dealing with the heart, and that was why the nurse gave me a pill.

He paced back and forth in the room, in the dark, grunting. With the light coming in from the gap under the door, I could see his silhouette—he looked muscular. I was terrified. Luckily, the medicine settled in, and I slept until the middle of the night when I was woken up by the nurse, who had taken my arm and strapped it with a monitoring band to check my vitals. They had to do this for the first five days. As I went back to sleep, I looked at the bed next to me and saw that it was empty. I looked around the room, and he was no longer there. I felt cold.

The next day I found out that the heroin addict jumped the fence. He didn't need to, one of the counselors had mentioned. He could have left at any time through the door—anyone could leave whenever they wanted.

That night, I was alone in the room, and again, I was given the pill, but my anxiety—my fear of so many unknowns—fought against the sedative effects. I didn't want to be with my thoughts—I had let so many people down in so many ways. I was so scared and depressed, the guilt—all of it, made the room darker. I didn't know how to cry that night.

I was already missing the heroin addict. Even though we never said a word to each other or acknowledged each other's presence in any way, he was company. He kept me from thinking. I stayed awake until the nurse came in to check my numbers. It wasn't until the next day that I was able to really sleep again—I had slept the whole day, not even realizing that the nurse had come in a few times to monitor my vitals.

I would think about him from time to time—he would randomly pop into my head. I was surprised how much he consumed my thoughts, for someone I had never interacted with aside from sharing a room for one night in rehab without any communication. I can still hear his grunts and the sound of his pacing. I wouldn't recognize him if we were to cross each other's paths—I hope, every day, that he made it—that maybe he was able to find help again, and that he was able to become clean. That's what recovery is all about—hoping, praying, wishing that we all will make it whether we know each other or not because no matter what, we all share an addiction—a burden that no one else would ever understand, and that was what brought us all closer, an understanding of each other's brain.

I remember, during one of our sessions, hearing that only 1 out of 10 of us won't relapse within the first three months of leaving rehab. I remember we all looked at each other—who knew what we all were thinking, the statistics were against us, and I remember hearing that roughly 60% of us won't make it through a year without giving in. Sometimes I think about how far I've come, sometimes I think about how far I have to go—either way, it's one day at a time—and the heroin addict's silhouette in the room that night will always be a reminder—a reminder that no matter what, if you look close enough, there can be a little light coming in from under the door and into the darkness.

Last Call
Jaywalker
(just walk away)

Needle In The Hay
+
the one in my brain

When Once I Was Gone

CHOCOLATE THIS and chocolate that—I taste until the soothing goes away. Run one mile, run two miles, run twenty miles. I go until the soothing releases. Read this, write that, laugh a little, cry a lot—my emotions seek to let go of the soothing (or whatever).

Soothe and soothe and soothe. Relinquish and regain. The past days are not to forget, but I can't remember anyway. And the way the cigarette puffs drift up toward the moon, thinking about loneliness and the difference between that and being alone, which I won't ever figure out—I don't think, at least, because I know no better. At least for now. At least for back then. At least for never.

And there is nothing wrong with not knowing—I hear there can be no reckoning with the fear of the unknown. And there was once a time when I had it all, but all was nothing to be had, come to find out, because all was nothing but a facade into escaping from the unknown.

Who knows.

Chocolate this and chocolate that.

Sugar addiction—that's a start. There's a start. Right?

I'll have an iced mocha, two chocolate chip cookies, a brownie, and a small carton of chocolate milk.

Then I'll order a dessert, please. Thanks.

Transitions and transferences.

I'll run it off a year from now, I would like to think. At some point.

The voices in my head are strangers to me, ones I've never met before and will never know until I say hi. Or maybe bye.

Once upon a time, a million years ago I took a sip—a long sip that found its way. It found its way while I lost mine. There was no life—just that sip and my own broken world. Thus.

Saying goodbye was what I was best at. I never said it. I just left. I never came back and I'll never want to go back. Want.

To let go, to give in to patience, to come to terms with the intersections of the past, future, and present—crossroads full of scars and lights.

Chocolate this and chocolate that. Immersed in the space between the texts, I hide and close my eyes so that the world feels closer. Closed.

Still trying to figure out which works best. Still trying to take it one day at a time. Still expecting the worst. Maybe one day it'll change. All that I know is that I'm here now, when once I was gone.

A Kolkata Dream

Consider a single cloud—angry and scowling, drifting away and bobbing up and down, almost like it's in the ocean trying to reach the horizon, and how dark and maddened, by itself amid plains of skies, giving home to avian flocks who pierce through this lone cloud without hesitation or thought. Upon fields and fields of endless minds, this lost scorned billow, to remain unfound—to exist as such as one only wants to—in reckless fury.

Consider your dead uncle who at the age of 99 hoped that he wouldn't make it to the turn of the century—how mad he was when he heard the fireworks thunder above Kolkata and his eyes, still open and unsatisfied. And when he finally passed, you smiled and looked at photographs from years ago, remembering his hopeful voice of wanting to no longer be alive—a teacup and a handkerchief—the wisdom in the walking cane, step after step into knowledge now no longer.

Consider the River Ganges: its glittered dhotis and saris floating with stray wooden boats, a hole here, a hole there—a rickshaw in the distance, in search of vanilla ice cream, perhaps, and how they bathed and soaped their garments—a cleansing, a ritual, the birth of evening as the sun descended and dissolved just beyond the edge of your tongue. You listened to the current transform your thoughts into holy rays of silence.

So you looked to identify this cloud—the one that filled your skull with confusion and chaos, in search of a friend who lacked love and passion for this place, and in this place, to be slashed by lightning or to vibrate from its rumbling touch, the only touch you recognized in the dizzying rotation of land and mass. Let such sensations take you away and forget about currents shocking your streams for every thought about the pains of each and every continent.

So you saw that child tucked away into a construction pipe as large as the vehicle that shakes along with the uneven streets of Kolkata, stuck in traffic—for every horn, there was progress, for every gesture and nod, there was an understanding that we might reach our destination but the seconds minutes hours were just figments of a taunting dream. Who was that with him—this baby? Maybe a brother or a sister—maybe they seek shelter from the summer heat, or perhaps it was their home for the time being, and you couldn't help but to think about catalytic converters and air conditioning and why you felt so lost and how they, those two, seemed so comfortable and at ease in such a metallic refuge.

So the morning conchs sounded amid the chatter of crows—the rise of day, and how you would look out the window to see a misty city on the brink of its beginnings. You, on the balcony of your grandfather's balcony, a bucket of marigolds next to you, strung along the railings, freshly washed cloths—its aroma ventured and mixed into the sounds of sizzling fish, for an early lunch. Below, cricket on a thin stretch of grass, wickets and rocks, and the murmuring thuds of the game quietly blend in with the waking city.

Consider this cloud—haunted and in search of peace now, and now no longer a desire for misery. To make amends with love all around—the love it rejected since the origin of earth or you. Able now, to cover and let be all that lives below, and consider how, in recognition of its own flaws, to become malleable, and float in harmony with that which it didn't know. Let it be and let it go—this dark bale of sky.

So evening's breath—the glowing huts of smoke and fire, and you'd walk around as night arrived, the air lit by cooks. There was a cart where one was selling books, and you stopped to see the collection. Your eyes stinging—you continued walking and let the natural Kolkata ragas consume you. Not so much lost anymore, you consider a single cloud and how it left without a word, and you were left alone in the middle of a Kolkata dream, where there was always a shine a gleam a glimmer because there was always hope—a hope to live and die and a hope to be reborn.

I'll Never Know

Dear Monica,

My name is Shome Dasgupta, and I just wanted to see if you'd be up for taking a look at a flash fiction piece I recently wrote. It's called "I'll Never Know" (670 words), and this one is really important to me—though it's fiction, it's also a narrative I experienced not too long ago, and to make sense out of it all, I had to shift it into words, I guess. It doesn't make that much sense, to be honest, so I just wrote it as fiction—I don't know.

Just in case you're curious what really happened, as it relates to the story—on a recent Sunday, while I was marveling at a heron soaring toward the sun, I happened to be stabbed in the shoulder. After overcoming the sharp twisting pain, I looked over and saw a knife—a glorious knife, indeed. Glistening—shiny and pretty, and the handle was a strong wood, carved in decor that looked very similar to a turtle I once saw in a ditch when I was a child. My brother and I loved ditches. I remember the turtle because it had three legs and welcoming eyes. I didn't want to miss the heron flying away, so I had to take a quick break from looking at the knife in my shoulder to become hypnotized again by these wings which—I don't know how else to explain it, but they were like wings full of wisdom—like when I looked at this bird, barely in the bright air, I felt its feathers inside my throat and its beak in my stomach—almost.

There was blood. I was becoming dizzy, and the knife was

still stuck in my shoulder. I don't know, Monica—I wanted to keep the blade there—it was in pretty deep, and the handle was so gorgeous, one that could've been on display in a museum. It felt like it was supposed to be there, you know—like in my shoulder? This knife—firm and careful—this heron of the air, and then with all of that going on, I literally saw a really bright butterfly hovering just before me—it felt like a friend. I put out my palm, and sure enough, the butterfly rested on my fingertip. The heron was gone by now—an echo in the sun—and I was still bleeding, and the butterfly took off, fluttering around my hand for just a bit—then it landed on the handle of the knife for like a second before making its way into the rest of the sky.

This was my left shoulder, so I put my right hand on the wood of the knife and grazed my skin against the carving—it took me back—it really did, and I found myself in the front yard of my childhood home, where in this photograph, my brother was trying to help me get on my bike. I miss him, Monica. As that picture flickered in and out under the haze of the sun—the blood settled in, and I had to lie down for a bit as the kayak caressed the basin—there was a whisper, and there it was—everything—it was all before me as I looked up into the sky. I don't even know what I saw, but it was all there before me, and I no longer felt the blade's warmth. I just saw it all.

Please note that this is a simultaneous submission, and I had previously sent a query to Eric over at *Flash Frog*, and he provided some really encouraging words, and he hopes that he'll be able to read this story one day. Maybe one day—who knows? Let's see how it goes—let's see how it all takes place. Maybe, I guess—it's why I'm reaching out to you.

Anyway, Monica—can I send this story your way? I understand if it isn't a fit and all, but I just thought I'd give it a try. I really don't know what happened, and I guess I'll never know.

Sincerely,
shome dasgupta

Coming Up Roses
moon

King's Crossing
(don't let me get)

Remember Nothing

The way the night looked, it looked like a massive hole was drilled into the sky. And the sun was gone. And the moon was covered. No stars. He looked up into the darkness and saw nothing. And nothing was fine. That was all he ever wanted. To see nothing. He used to close his eyes to see nothing, but that night, he didn't have to.

It was on that night when he decided to give it all away. All of his possessions. His house, his car, his TV—everything. He stared into the ocean of blackness and realized that this was what he wanted.

"I want nothing."

The next day, he put up his house for sale, including all that was inside. He put up his car for sale. He quit his job.

"What are you going to do?" his friend asked, a childhood friend and now former colleague.

"Nothing."

Once all that he had owned was sold, he lived on the streets as a homeless man. He had a homeless friend and they talked about nothing, and that was all he ever wanted.

One day his friend and former colleague—a friend since childhood—came up to him and gave him some money.

"I miss you," his friend said. "Come back."

He didn't respond, and after a minute or so, his friend walked away. He watched him walk and thought about nothing.

His homeless companion asked him, "Who was that?"

"He's nothing," he said.

That night the rain came down, large cold drops falling upon his body. He didn't seek cover. He sat there in the rain and thought about how much he loved the rain—he thought about how much he loved her and nothing.

"This is nothing."

It was a thunderstorm, and the night was loud. There was lightning. And across from where he sat, drenched and happy about nothing, he saw a building catch on fire after being struck by lightning.

The building was ablaze, pure fire. It was the building where his wife used to work. She no longer existed. She was nothing.

He stared at the building covered in light, the raindrops fell, the thunder was there, and there was the lightning. He sat there. He sat there and remembered. He remembered when his wife was alive. He remembered the touch of her skin, her voice. He remembered her kindness and compassion. He remembered her smile and the way she slept. He remembered. He remembered her last day.

The building burned. He sat there and watched it before it was washed out. He went to sleep. The next day was bright and fresh. The air was cool. He woke up and looked at the remains of the building.

"It's nothing now," he said. "Nothing is nothing. And nothing is fine."

His homeless friend, who had sought shelter during the storm, came back and asked him what happened.

"Nothing," he said.

He closed his eyes and let the shiny day press upon his face.

His friend, his childhood friend and former colleague, came back to give him some money—he did this daily.

"I'm sorry," his friend said.

"It's nothing."

As he watched his friend walk away, he thought about everything. And everything was the past, and everything was just memories. And his memories were everything—and his wife was everything.

"I miss you," he said.

"What's that?" his homeless friend asked.

"Nothing."

Before he moved to another place—it would be his last move—he had one last memory of her. He remembered. They were sitting on the grass of their front yard. It was midnight and it was raining, and the night was pure and dark and starless. There was no sky. And they talked about everything and nothing. It was the night before she died. And it was his last memory before going. And it was everything and nothing. And he smiled before going.

I Want to See the Music of Your Dreams

During my first time in an ambulance, I wasn't sure if my brother was alive, or if he was unconscious, or if he was just being really quiet. Just before the accident, I was reading Ovid's *Metamorphoses* in the front passenger seat. I had come home late the night before from playing in a JV basketball game, which was about an hour away from home, and I needed to catch up on some homework. And the last thing I had heard was my brother cursing and then the truck hit us, and there was smoke and glass and blood and burnt rubber. Sunny Day Real Estate was no longer playing.

When I opened my eyes—or rather, when I opened my left eye—I saw a face telling me that everything will be okay and that an ambulance was on its way. I was never able to meet that man or find out his name, but I will always remember his face and soothing voice. I could make out that our friends who were in the car were doing okay, but I kept calling my brother's name and he never responded. I kept calling his name in the ambulance and still nothing. And for some reason, I started singing Cracker's "Low"—the chorus part—and I sang it over and over again, perhaps because I loved that song, and the first time I had heard it was in the car with my brother, on the way to school. Much of the music I appreciated back then, and now, had come from listening to my brother's music collection like

Sebadoh, Pavement, Outkast, Sunny Day Real Estate, Wu-Tang Clan, The Olivia Tremor Control, 2Pac, Beck, and of course, Cracker. This was during the mid-'90s.

I kept singing that one line over and over until I heard my brother's voice. He said my name. I stopped singing and started crying. I stopped crying and started singing again to keep my brother awake. If anything, surely my horrible, out-of-pitch voice could keep him up. I still think about that ride in the ambulance, and how, when I thought death was near, I went straight to music for help, for a hand to run through my hair and lips to kiss me on the cheek. It was the first time I reached for music during a time other than when feeling my usual high school angst: *I'm depressed, no one understands, she or he won't love me, I have no friends*. This was something different—I didn't know if my brother was alive.

When we got home, I couldn't go to school for a few days—my right eye was patched up due to abrasion, and the right side of my face was scraped red and raw. My brother had a wrap around his left leg, and his face was full of sorrow—showing a pain that I'm sure hurt more than his physical ailment—from seeing me the way I was, post-accident. I still wonder what he was thinking about when he looked at me that week.

Even then, while in bed, watching TV through my left eye, I only kept the channel on VH1, watching videos—like Joan Osborne's "One Of Us" and Jewel's "Who Will Save Your Soul"—over and over again. Even today, every now and then, I'll listen to their CDs while driving, to thank them for keeping me company at a time when I felt vulnerable and out of place.

The second time I was in an ambulance, it was 2003. I had

been taken straight from the Lafayette Regional Airport to the hospital—I was just getting back from India, having dysentery, a twisted appendix, and volatile back spasms that made me scream so much on the flight from Houston to Lafayette that the flight attendant called for an ambulance while en route and asked the pilot to speed up to get me safely to a hospital. Again, I didn't know her name—but I still remember her face and voice, and I'm extremely thankful for her concern. During the remainder of that flight, I even had those cliché flashbacks of my parents and my grandparents smiling at me, and there was one of my brother and me playing in the back yard with Elliott Smith playing in the background. On this ambulance ride, Radiohead's "Bullet Proof... I Wish I Was" played in my head, and in between my shouting, I remember thinking what a great last song to hear before passing on.

I like to write. I like to read and watch movies and plays and pretend to know how to play the guitar, but when I think someone I love is in pain or when I'm in pain, I seek music's hand. It's something I only realized lately. I can't play any instruments. I never got past playing the first few seconds of Weezer's "Undone—The Sweater Song," and I can't sing at all. But I love how none of that matters. How in the end, I will most probably be singing some random lyrics while reliving moments of my life and remembering the ones I love.

Her Garden Her Earth

THERE WAS a dying garden under a rising sun, and the way the light came through, I closed my eyes and wondered about darkness shone upon by beams of such magnitude that I became confused about the difference between love and loneliness—a twilight it was, where the edge of the world thinned into ghosts floating around in my mind. I still saw her. Her knees covered and caked with soil, knuckles scraped and torn, and next to her, a chipped spade as if missing a tooth. She patted earth with weathered palms, her earth, where she only knew how to exist, the only realm she wanted to be, among the dirt and minerals—clay was her only companion.

And so her hair covered her face—she whispered words I would hear at night, when we were alone. Those words were never meant for me and I knew that. My love would never weaken but only strengthen when she was gone. When she left, the sky was cut in half, down through the center of earth, and that was where she was taken away. Not from me but to her earth—her wishes became true, not a cry or a grunt or a shout of pain but a smile as she traveled to her destination under the plates where I stood, heaved breath I recollected the fury of leaves and roots—her gravestone of flushed vines I tried to grasp with memories of when she was here.

2:45 AM

Candles and Petals

He was a mama's boy with a mouth full of trash. It wasn't a complete sentence for him unless the word "fuck" was in it, and it wasn't a complete day if he didn't tell his mom that he loved her.

Not too many people liked Daylen—mainly because they didn't know Daylen, or they were rather intimidated by him. He was covered in tattoos, and he covered his face in a hoodie or a baseball cap, and wore sagging khaki pants and a white undershirt, and his face was always scruffy, covering some of the scars he had gotten growing up—from fights usually. But the fights weren't necessarily his fault, as most of the time, he was defending himself or his mother.

His mother was the town drunk—she had been so for as long as Daylen could remember. At the age of four, he learned how to hold his mom's hair back when she was sick from drinking too much, and then it wasn't too much longer—a handful of years later—when he had to learn how to drive to pick his mother up from jail or the corner of whatever street where there was a bar or at some random guy's house. He would sit on a stack of magazines just so he could see over the steering wheel while also using a branch to use the accelerator or the brakes.

Carrie was her name, and no matter what, just before she would pass out, Daylen would tell her that he loved her, whether she would hear it or not.

"You're too good to me," she would say sometimes, when she

was half-coherent.

"I love you, Ma," Daylen would reply. "Now get some sleep and I'll make you some fucking pancakes when you wake up. Love you, Ma."

Daylen's boyfriend, Brent, was quite the opposite of Daylen, physically speaking. He always tucked his shirt in, combed his hair, and he didn't have any tattoos; rarely did he curse. His skin wasn't as dark as Daylen's, looking pale—even during the summertime.

They met in the parking lot of one of the local shops—Daylen had just bought his mom some flowers, a bouquet of sunflowers, when he bumped into two older men who were verbally attacking him about his mom, calling her a whore, and saying how they both slept with her, and it was the worst they ever had.

The verbal arguments then turned into a fight, and Daylen managed to get in a few solid hits, but in the end, the two men were able to catch Daylen in a hold, trading punches. Brent saw the fight and rushed over, taking a couple of hits himself before successfully breaking it up. He helped Daylen to his feet, and that was the beginning of their relationship. Four months later, they admitted their love for each other, and they were inseparable since then.

After a four-day drinking binge, Carrie returned home late at night—the house was dimly lit, candles everywhere—rose petals surrounded the kitchen table and the sink was full of cooking equipment, plates, and glasses.

"Hey, Ma," Daylen said. "I fucking missed you, Ma. Are you okay?"

"Hey, baby," Carrie replied as she held onto anything and

everything, making her way to the living room couch—she fell onto it.

Daylen helped her to position herself so that her face wasn't planted into the cushion.

"Ma," Daylen whispered, as he brushed her hair aside. He used his shirt to wipe off the smeared makeup.

"Ma," Daylen whispered. "I just got fucking engaged, Ma. Me and B, Ma."

"Do you have a cigarette?"

Daylen pulled out a cigarette and lit it for her.

"Look, Ma—fucking candles and petals and everything."

His mom coughed, which turned into a coughing spasm, and Daylen sat her up, rubbing her back.

"You're too good to me, honey," she said, as the smoke wavered over her face.

Daylen took the cigarette from her mouth.

"Get some sleep, Ma," he said. "And I'll fucking make some fucking pancakes for you in the morning. Love you, Ma."

She closed her eyes, and he kissed her on the forehead before gently positioning her body so that she could sleep on the couch.

The next morning, before he left to meet Brent at the coffee shop, he made his mother some pancakes and left a note for her on the kitchen table. As he walked across town, he found himself in another fight, and this time Brent wasn't there to help him. All he could think about, with each punch, each kick, each elbow, as he was on the ground getting hit, was sipping lattes with his fiancé and holding Brent's hand while his mother was eating pancakes at home in the kitchen.

In the Shadow of a Bird

THE FIRST TIME I stood and walked over to the podium to share at an AA meeting, I talked about plate tectonics—meaning I had no clue what I was saying as I hadn't studied geography or earth sciences since seventh grade, and all I could remember that day in that room full of Styrofoam cups of coffee was mentioning earthquakes and aftershocks and lands shifting—finding a balance, however temporary, perhaps, and how it relates to life. Now 45 months into sobriety, I think about that last line in Modest Mouse's "Bankrupt On Selling" and how when *The Lonesome Crowded West* first came out in 1997—my sophomore year in high school—I listened to that song for the first time and it became my favorite song, but I didn't really know the meaning of it until roughly 20 years later. I can't remember the last time I listened to those lyrics—it has been awhile, definitely before my sobriety, and it still pops into my head as I drive around Lafayette so randomly it's as if I had listened to it all day, a one-track compilation, over and over and over. Little did I know.

45 was the number Michael Jordan chose to use when he returned to the NBA for his second run of the three-peat. He ended up changing it back to 23, and for his last game with the Bulls—to win his sixth championship—he hit the game-winning shot over with Brian Russell or Byron Russell. He scored 45 points that game, evoking this surreal, circular nature of life with an unexpected meaning of numbers. My friend and I were juniors then, and we were at his house, which was built

on a prominent golf course in Broussard, where every now and then golf balls would rattle around the back porch, and we sat at the coffee table at the center of the living room eating Blue Bell mint chocolate chip ice cream. This was after a dinner of homemade lasagna, and after the game had finished, we went out to the driveway and shot hoops under the garage floodlights. I remember the echo of each dribble was extra that night—louder than usual, and it was summer in the Deep South, so we were sweating and giddy and it was that moment, years later, that I realized I had the best bowl of mint chocolate chip ice cream ever in my life.

That friend, now a friend of 35 or so years—when we graduated from high school, it was the first time we had been separated since first grade. He went off to college in another state, and I stayed here in Lafayette—I always stayed here and I still hold my mother's hand when I cross the street, and everyone I grew up with left around then, and I found myself living in the same world but with unfamiliar faces. Three years into college, here at the University of Louisiana at Lafayette, a hurricane landed, and when the electricity goes out, the darkness hits with a thud—it's a different kind of darkness, one that overwhelms any existence of hope. During these times, I realize that unfamiliar faces are lit in the shadows of thunder and violent rains, as if we're holding hands without ever lifting our arms. The bare necessities become the most important needs, and the first thought that always enters my mind is that when this is all over with—when the quiet settles in, I want to find out who played Casey Jones in *The Teenage Mutant Ninja Turtles* movie because whenever I was growing up, renting this movie from the local video store—later on buying the VHS—it was Casey who always let me know that it's okay to be a friend to someone you may never know. Now, Raphael was always my favorite because all in all, he was the one who had it the toughest, and he was able to make it through by the end.

In the end, my mother makes a rather rude curry—whether it's chicken or eggplant, and when our home is filled with seasoning and sizzling and when my mind tickles a bit with each tongue, I find myself missing my family's origins—India, where the dogs of the streets teach us about humility and survival, perhaps, letting us know that there is something holy in the dirt. Sometimes, when I pass through the kitchen, I turn around to see if I'm being followed by a pup with ribbed skin and sunken teeth, and when I don't see one, I can imagine these powerful eyes—eyes that could only be felt through the daggers of pain and fire. There is no one who loves my brother more than me, and I don't know if he'll ever know that—let alone anyone else— but I love him so much that it's overwhelming, so I keep it to myself until a day comes, such as a day when I call him from rehab after my own world shattered into tears of glass and blurred visions of remnants of a lost mind to hear that sibling voice born of the same skin and breath, knowing that no matter what, there is a prototype better suited for an earth. When we were young and our father took us to the video shop—Raccoon Records—we didn't go to the new releases or browse around; we went to the same movies over and over again, movies like *Willow* or *The NeverEnding Story* or *Who Framed Roger Rabbit*. It was in such movies I found kinship with emotions and imagination.

The first two movies which I remember making me cry were

Dead Poets Society and *Batman*—both released in 1989. The former I watched at a cousin's house when the family was visiting Vancouver and Edmonton, the birthplaces of my brother and me, respectively, and the latter I watched at the movie theater in the Acadiana Mall. I can't remember which one I saw first or which one made me cry first because tears and time blend together in an infinite memory. What is a feeling without knowing its opposite? That's why the soundtrack to *Amélie* brings me so much joy—to find joy in sitting at the single table at the corner of the coffee shop pretending to exist as I shine the biggest smile on my face with those thick headphones, the ones audio professionals wear at a soundboard. I could feel the smile in its fullest essence—stretched skin, a jaw without fixed hinges, and when a friend walked by, he said he could see my smile from across the room. My only vivid memory of visiting New York when I was 15 is the two-story Sbarro, and it was the first time I folded a pizza. Memory can be fickle and it can be misleading—either way, however lacking it can be, in its dearth there is a truth that leads to multiple sensations, spanning the spectrums of a universe found in a mind.

I don't know if I've talked to an actual ghost or seen one, but I don't think it matters, because the experience itself is where I find purpose—what I once thought was a squirrel edging a green field was just a shadow of a bird flying in a blue sky. I feel like it's much easier to talk out loud to yourself when no one is around than when you're surrounded by people. I feel like it's easier to talk out loud to yourself when you're surrounded by people than when you're by yourself. Either way, there's an attempt to communicate and in its failure, there is a stretch of light. A light that might flicker or remain constant, and all that matters for me is that there is some kind of light. Then, for me, there's a chance—there's a chance that I might be able to learn more about plate tectonics and geography and how the land can bend and crack and topple over and find a balance to where we can remain steady and look ahead, whether we're stumbling or otherwise, and in those moments, we can look back and find those small moments of our lives that will forever hover in our minds until we find a hand stretched out to help us find a piece of still land—and when we turn our heads back, all that we can see are familiar faces, faces created for us.

Waltz #2

(but)

I don't know you
I love you
Cathy's Clown
Alphabet Town
ABCDE
FGHIJ
KLMN
OPQRST
UVWXYZ
I'll show you around

Rickshaw Wrench and Spoke

SELDOM DAYS anyway, they took it upon themselves to care—rare was the occasion they showed up to see the world, mostly huddled in a corner, where there was no light, perfectly content with a glass of water, a piece of bread, and a ragged blanket. But sometimes, there was an innate calling to reveal their magnitude to earth—perhaps some would feel the lands shake and tumble while others kept their eyes closed and covered their ears.

Once, skies darkened—turmoiled, as if volcanic spout—clouds so ghostly they hummed about loss as they twirled about in rage and sadness. This was a day they ventured from their corner—they, in shreds and scraps, bumped bones and weathered scars—barefoot they strolled to recognize the makings of a day as they forgot about time and the meaning of sun and moon. A wind with force—they leaned their heads forward to push through just for a glance.

So we are destitute—so we are the ones not to be greeted, for their disgust for us knows no boundaries.

Ashed skies and torn air, they continued as they wondered if they should return to their shelter of tin plates and grains. No love for what they found in a world of no embrace, they glanced here and there, nodded and shook, grimaced and scoffed at their view. And spheres thundered and cracked; electric as it was, they enjoyed the performance—dried lands before them, barren and hungered—they walked upon surfaces jagged and strayed, only to smile at thoughts of home where light was always welcomed but never entered.

So why such a life, so why such a world, so why are they here for such is the way we need not. Let us go let us go. Let the monsoons have their way—there is no argument.

And they turned back with winds in full support, the skies so heavy and sulked, they watched their way to cause no disturbance. But, there—a plea, a whimper, that of which only they could hear and receive. Upon strained glimpse to see a tattered rickshaw bent as if elderly, and beside it, a little one—a ragged little one—wrench in hand and spoke. With scraped skin and dirty brow, the little one clenched a wheel with teeth and grunted.

And so they pondered over to inquire about such activity and task.

Little one, oh little one—why?

With that the child replied.

Please and please, my father's rickshaw has fractured—can't you see and look? The storm is here, my sister away, I must to pick her up and bring home safely.

Still curious and in wonder, they continued to ask.

But why do you bite this wheel and not use this wrench? Are you hungry, child?

The ragged little one in tears—red eyes and bruised face, he answered.

I know not what else to do.

Vibrated lands the wind blew, with that, brought in such rain and confusion for the day was unexpected for all, including them and one. Without a word, they took the wrench and spoke and wheeled it all together with squint eyes and hard breath, that which unheard in fury of monsoon's wake—racket and clash went earth, a time of no hesitance. Like that and that, the wheel and spoke attached, a rickshaw no longer unable to carry on its infinite burden.

With glee and joy and shouts deafened by split skies, the little one embraced them and pattered away in puddles and rocks to find sister and bring her back home to family. Them—they viewed a large pipe, rust and mud—they entered for shelter and there they slept, such loud banging lulled them asleep and how they dreamt of their corner of the world, their own home—with smiled lips they looked forward to their return as if they had never left.

Photospheric Magnifications

Suppose that they as siblings as they were and they peered over jagged and caked mud, dried and powdered—a polished creek, shined and silver—and saw splintered sun as reflections of their eyes and heads. What were they to think upon such transparency where their faces dissolved with sculpin scale and streamed hush of river thinned and slept? To imagine otherwise would distort and entwine, and softly they transformed into glowed balloons of red or yellow or peach dependent on day's tenure. Their locks and curls straightened and ironed—rays like shimmered mills twirled and cut as such into air, and air they lifted above and hand in hand they rose with fitted clasp. Consider a thought of goose and stork and crane to play witness upon flight and crossed paths in vertical manner to view these strangers as mirage and magic. Perhaps a sounded beak of awe or ponder, to tilt their feathers aside before dive and nest—the stories to be told to their clutch and brood on horizon's eve. Conglomerates they became, sibling and sibling as celestial bond they floated to star's reach, whereupon they gathered their sight and found the world below, a pebble in galactic ratio, how they would to place in their shredded pockets or their tongues atop. And so with keen and curious eyes they saw upon a palace of wood and nails, their mother and father lost from their lives amid storm and thunder, and with pined pleas and helium tears they left from sun's shredded limb to soar as meteorites through a maze of constellations and dust and gently landed aside. Hand in hand again, they lay their simmered heads against familiar chests and wished for breath and heave. Ventured in, a blanket flower from raised wind's mouth, they each took and placed on bark and mound and closed their eyes to dream of voice and laughter under lowered sun, their only friend.

Acorns of Memories

A BITTEN MOON looked over him as he licked acorns in search of his sister. There was dew and the palate of dirt with each lick brought a memory—each lick so painful, so wonderful, so magical, every acorn that touched his tongue became of pebbles as if planted in a riverbed before history existed. Earth settled against the inner walls of his mouth, a cave full of grit, and his sister, in flashes, would simmer throughout his body. There they were—standing between two bronze bales of hay in a field full of dandelions, holding yellow and orange balloons, as if to mirror the set sun—a celebration of their birth. There they were—creating currents in the pond, moss drooped over, splashing each other and teaching one another how to multiply in their heads using the number of times each of them had been stung by wasps. *8. 6. 48.* And there they were, in their shared room, wooden floor, cold air, she in her bed—a soaked wash-cloth on her forehead as he held her frozen hand and sang a lullaby about shovels and watermelons. *Sing to me about the way the blisters mounded on our palms.* He put three more acorns in his mouth and juggled them around like the marbles in their hands when he and his sister played stars of the universe out on the porch drizzled by mosquitoes under a flickering lantern. Eyes closed tight—the humid air pressed heavy on the back of his neck, he closed his eyes tighter, hurting his own skull—a jawbone of no release. There they were—on their backs, fingers pointing toward a tilted sky as they counted sparrows and clouds.

3. 4. 5. 12. 13. His mouth now, cheeks puffed and pierced with acorns, he swiveled his cut tongue around, in search for more of her—throwing pecans in a rusted bucket placed on top of a wheel-less tractor, speckled with feathers and ants. And he opened his eyes and there she was—in land, amidst the soil—her new world under the stars of the universe. *Let us play. Let us play. Let us play.* He spat out the acorns and called out her name and cried, crying so loud the roots of the oak looked sad and soft. And so he lay on his back and looked at the night glittered through branches and there came a smile. He reached for another acorn and licked it and let the moon fall on his eyes.

Barlow and Chelsea

Barlow opened the door (he saw Chelsea standing in front of him; he said hello, but he didn't know what else to say—he hadn't seen her in eight years, since she had moved to France or England of Spain; he could tell, by the way she didn't look into his eyes, that she knew he was in love with her; Barlow thought about what he should say next—he told her that he twisted his ankle yesterday; he stepped aside and watched Chelsea walk toward the freezer).

A Slight Tremor

THE RIVER was cracking and shifting—I assumed the plates below must have been churning to cause such an event, and between the lightning strikes I could see fish dying to become humans—the icy water was suffocating them, turning their gills into frozen window panes, and I felt the ground trembling as the plates were adjusting so I ran to the pitcher's mound of the nearby baseball park, thinking that it would be the best place to be for an earthquake—it wasn't too dramatic though and I wasn't scared, and it didn't last too long—after the world stopped moving, I stood and ran back to the riverbank to look for the turtle with the portrait of Van Gogh on its shell.

Rose Parade
(follow me down)
Fond Farewell

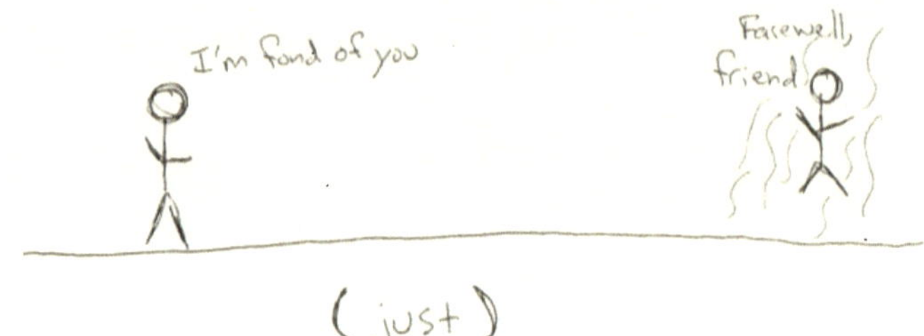
I'm fond of you
Farewell, friend
(just)

The Sisters

THEY BREATHED mud—the sisters, every Sunday.

They snuck out of the church—through the back—and ran as fast as they could to the pond. Holding hands, they ran circles around the water, and when they started to pant, they dropped down and put their faces into the ground. Closing their eyes, they inhaled mud. They breathed it in, letting the soaked dirt into their nostrils and fill their brains with clay. They tasted it. They stuck their tongues into earth and moved them around until they were gritty and brown.

Then they lifted their heads and looked at each other—their teeth were no longer white, and their eyebrows were clumped and hardened. Again they stuck their heads back into the earth and laughed and sang songs until their lungs were full of land and worms.

When the service was over—sounded by the chimes of a bell, the sisters stood up, with their discolored pink and white dresses, sagging and squishy, and jumped into the pond, trying to catch as many lily pads as possible, knowing that they would be grounded for another week. It didn't bother them; they never complained—they knew they were always allowed to go back to church.

Signs of Communication

"This is your final warning. The warranty for your automobile will expire, and there is due attent—."

"Hello—hello. Hello. Please, hello."

He heard the phone disconnect, and he looked around his room—bare, empty—deserted.

Silence—just silence. He waited. There was no weather. There was no time. There was no one—there was no language. There was no world. He waited.

"This is your fin—."

"Hi. Hello. I'm here—I'm here. Please don't go."

There was more of nothing.

On his bed crouched forward with his elbows on his knees, a head to the dust of the wooden floors, as if there was a prayer. More time or nothing—four walls, a creation of hollow samples of strangled lines. A day upon a day, he felt a torment. On the table, just even with a pillow without dents or creases, sat a container of aloe lotion, a brush, and a sparkling watch. Every now and then, he almost turned his head toward the other side—the side that was no longer there.

52 years.

"Hi—hi. Yes. I'm here."

"This is to inform you that there's a lawsuit pending against—."

"That's wonderful. What should I do? It would be my pleasure."

"—action is required."

"Please. I'm here. Please don't."

He said this, only to a click.

Indeed, there was hope.

"Greetings. We're calling to let you know that your house and all of your assets have been repossessed due to recent acquisitions. Be advised that—."

"Yes. Who is this? I am here. I can talk. Please talk to me. I have no one to talk to—I'm here."

"Any disputes can be claimed through your local—."

"Take my hand, dear."

Another ended call—a one-way conversation, and he again was in his room, stuck with the echoes of his own mind. He couldn't turn around. On his own side of the bed, on the table, an empty glass—there for as long as the blanket never moved. There, for as long as a toothbrush remained still every morning and every night.

This was it. This will be it, he thought, as the back of his neck was rigid, aching. It was ringing, but he dropped it—falling, he scrambled on the floor, picking up the phone, like an aged map for treasure, lost for a million years only to be found tucked in the dresser drawer of an abandoned home hidden in the ruins of nowhere.

A different sound—a different tone every time, and every time, he wished for it to be someone, anyone, to say hello—to talk about the day.

"Hello—."

"Hi. How are you doing? What would you like for breakfast?"

"I'm—and I'm here to let you know—."

"Would you like to go to the garden today?"

"It is too late to take any—."

"How about we go out for dinner, dear."

"If any matter arises, contact us—."

"The bees are outside again."

"This is your final notice—."

"Lemonade."

And that was it, and there was nothing else. That was the last time—he threw his phone against the wall, cracked and splintered. He picked it up and threw it again—again and again and again. There were no signs of communication, and as he gathered his thoughts and turned around, he looked at the far side of the bed—a still life, so it appeared.

He walked there and went under the cover—cold and tight, and he lay on his side, looking at the sparkling watch and the aloe cream next to it. He lay there and put his thumb in his mouth and closed his eyes, dreaming of a conversation that could never happen.

"I miss your voice."

Fission and Fusion

IN RAIN the drops sang down—fallen faces pressed against muddied windows. Who's to say that tears knew no difference between sun and moon—and the moon never turned around to look, to see that when covered in sheets and splintered skies, that we looked up for more.

A clearing: and so we looked up for more, in twilight prisms we oscillated, beamed as if the sun practiced magic and we, hypnotized, followed all laws of heat. When a day became hidden under our tongues, a cloud could find its way through our pores and seep in like fog over fields.

Siblings we were.

Siblings we were, and once there was magnolia before us—one we'd adventure from arm to arm, chipping bark with our ax teeth until we lost the touch of taste. Such the splendor, this magnolia, our skin eroded like history.

Then when sibling fell and broken neck, let loose the flock of redbirds, all hovered, they sang the song of sadness, such a magnolia it was, to play the harps and subtract one from the other. Here I was alone in holy matrimony.

Here I was alone, so it went, my own flock, fluttered about between the banks of my mind—I knew no more other than a whispered plea to combine sibling with me.

Up and up and up I went, a crawl upon such towering roots,

and up until I became foliage, my drops of dew from my eyes—
no song of sadness sang by feathers and wings. I became a king
of canopy and saw before me, sibling between sun and moon,
and there I went, from fission to fusion once again.

A Brief Introduction to Memory

Forever winter the day the story was told—and how the pretzeled sky twisted its way into their mouths to create such a stir that the sun blinked while all else kept their eyes opened in awe. In awe they were to hear soporific hums venturing in from a million years away, where there was no horizon but a light so loud the world knew there was no way to mute such brilliance. Such was the way the axis tilted in curious sadness and how their tongues stuck out as tremored sap vibrated against bark wondering when fossils will live again to account the tale of history. And how the light froze over, a glaze like frosted pond with stilled lily pads and ambered mosquitos, music blinding such that they knew not what to do other than to thank the hours unending for this unexpected spectacle.

They felt to long for the past, to be encapsulated and cozied in bubbles floating in sporadic fashion toward time where then they will anticipate the future and its ending. Those rainbow reflections pressed against oscillated spheres—their necks stretched so far to glimpse these ripples of foreshadowing. Little they knew, little they knew how existence would stupor to such levels where death created their lives, an awakening from within, new to sensations of breath and marbled chipped statues. And tears came down, each drop full of memories streaked against their faces to form thunder above their heads like halos of darkness—to wonder or to leave, to wander or to breathe—they hesitated to ponder future gleams, all else behind them like a forgotten path to jubilee.

Such sensations they felt, fingertips and touch and pores and pores soaked in morning moons they followed trances of howled teeth. Swayed branches covered in melted echoes brushed past their ears. Sounds of hunger wavered below their chins. On knees suppliants yearned to placate a ringing and hollowed bellows of pierced bronze blades stuck to the roofs of their throats. They closed their eyes and learned to remember.

A Distance of Thunder

So SIMMERED angelic melodies and ruins wrath, merged crumbled echoes to formed paths, gave way to screamed lullabies. They faced each other with mouths opened, full of silence and skies, a desire to counter inertia—to stop the world for a second, confuse time and gravity and torn ocean waves. To dissolve the moon with seasoned eyes, a distance of thunder grew between their palms, a hole of light found solace just above their brows, lifted chins toward magmatic flowed clouds—loud and ashed. A drift a split a crack to where no one journeyed unless shifted lands slanted and bent to lead them into a core of their own minds. There they found embraced statues of ice entwined as aged roots from eons ago when earth was earth and nothing else could feel other than leaves and stems drawn toward the sun. A magnetic pull never to be cleaved or weakened, these fossils frozen reminded them of skin and tranquility gave birth from beyond the sprinkled stars to where they sought knowledge of clasped hands and twisted necks, lips and breath of volcanic rupture. They learned to hold. The glaciers attached by lightning, tied by luminous streams, crashed and slowed—pushed together, a friction so heated it sparked touch and gleam. A twilight of morning rose to let them sing their song of dew and fire—this the love like no other, never to be witnessed but only by soared sacred beaks centuries from now.

Such Velocity

So THEY WALKED in fields of stalks as tall as them—hands grazed against bold leaves, of what will burn to sugar—ashes sing to clouds and skies. Their eyes made of water and deepened coughs to relax. They ran through sizzled mounds, blackened dirt they strode next to each other in hope of a clearing. Nebulous vanished, how they looked with amazed ponder. Such was the world and here they stood. They beheld an atmosphere, a pulse in wrists and ribs—a flushed sun. They shone and embraced flapped wings, a clasp so tight they found themselves in high air, swimmed cumulus, waded and force-bowed their heads to breathe. To look down and view earth with outward tongues, in tears they followed feathered rhythms and beaked murmurs. They wondered: to let go would mean forever separated, the two who had found love in a balloon amid planets unknown, never discovered. And with teeth clenched and gritted, in silence they departed as palms opened—they sifted azure as cloths shredded and ragged they became. Such velocity they went, eyes leveled parallel and planked. Farewell farewell. This, they returned to silt and matter. And so they fell in perpendicular fashion, down straight through crust and plate, speechless and a wave as if to say the worth of love was the worth of loss. For they were never lost; they knew no boundaries. And there they went, soft and quiet into a realm they had never seen before as ashed melodies floated and wandered, a harvest like no other.

Café, Three Times

I SEE YOUR sorrow-filled sighs, as you sit next to me at the café. I could open my lips and ask you what's wrong, but you look too tired to speak. The steam from your tea no longer rises, though the cup is full to the rim. Your shoelaces are untied; your hair is mangled. I take the last sip of my coffee and leave a tip on the table, but before I exit, I bend down and tie your shoelaces. That can be a start, I think, and walk out the door. I look through the window, but your head hasn't turned. Eight steps later, I go back into the café and untie your shoelaces. Thanks, you say to me, without moving your lips, without blinking or breathing. I nod and leave the coffee shop the third time that morning.

Say Hi

I HAVE THREE guitars, but I don't know how to play any of them—or rather I can play three chords, and I like to joke and say that I can play one chord for each guitar. I don't have any musical talent—I can't play any instruments, I can't sing, and I lack the patience and tenacity to overcome these shortcomings. I can't manipulate my fingers to the rhythms of the world, and my hypocrisy knows no bounds—I still would love to learn how to play the guitar and sing, yet I'm not doing anything about it.

My musical tastes run the gamut—including hip hop, indie, country, radio, jazz, blues, electronic—any and all of it. Whether I know a genre or style or not, I'm constantly in search of sound.

Sometimes I ask myself what medium of art affects me most emotionally, and I can never truly answer the question—whether it's a song or a written work, a show or a movie, a drawing or a painting—but whenever I ask myself what was it that really hypnotized me into writing, I think that I can pin it down to three experiences—one band and two books.

I still very vividly remember reading Judy Blume's *Tales Of A Fourth Grade Nothing* on a red recliner in our living room. I read it in one sitting, shifting my body left and right without taking my eyes off those pages.

Later on, one book and one band pretty much made their way to me around the same time. Sitting at a local coffee shop, I read Gabriel García Márquez's *Chronicle of a Death Foretold*—one of the author's shorter novels, a novella I guess—and it was my first book I read written by Márquez, and it didn't take much longer, after I became immersed in all of his works, that he became one of my most influential writers.

Right around the same time, I fell in love with the music of a Louisiana band known as Neutral Milk Hotel, particularly the songs "Two-Headed Boy, Pt. Two" and "Oh Comely," from the album *In the Aeroplane Over the Sea*. The rustic, the rural, the specters, and imagery—I was simply amazed by the visions created through words. I had always loved music, but now I fell in love with music.

Both Márquez and Neutral Milk Hotel—the way they molded their own worlds through tongue and tip, and how every sensation they produced was every sensation I wanted—I was enamored with it all.

These three points of a triangle, I think, formed the foundations for wanting to write—for wanting to create passions out of words, the lyrical or otherwise, to generate a feeling, an emotion which mirrored the feeling, an emotion that I experienced through these forms of imaginations.

To communicate or to fail in communication—and to do whatever it takes through sound and meaning and words to exhibit these metaphorical journeys and relatable realities—is what I think draws me to most forms of creativity. And the imagery of music certainly puts me in the trance I wanted to dive into whether I knew it or not.

The magical, the solitude, the attempts to reach out and communicate as a way to make some kind of sense or observation of what is going on around us, whether grounded in reality or in a ghost world so intangible we lift our hand to clasp hands with nothing—this wonder and weaving, the unwound and the wounded, all through arrangements and sounds—I strive to recreate these spectrums in an attempt to say hi.

Then there are the hip hop groups such as Wu-Tang and OutKast where I really felt the force of using language and twisting and turning it, building words upon words to offer symbolic meaning, however apparent or not, and how abiding by the usual constructs of writing is not needed at all, but rather it can be necessary to break those boundaries to help me search for those emotions I wanted to emit. To be a magician—to show how the trick is performed to the audience while actually performing the trick, pulling words out of a hat when all the words are already there before you—this was all so very entrancing and drew me closer and closer to the love of writing.

And Elliott Smith, too—who also exemplified for me the many ways to create a feeling I was most attracted to through lyrical storytelling. Sometimes it's not the actual meaning of the word that pulls me in, but rather it's the connotative energy that forms some kind of shield around me—and wanting to never leave this globe of colorful sensations that have become embedded in my mind.

Sometimes I don't want to understand the meaning of a song—I just want to let the song create a meaning for me. This sentiment goes for not only music, but for literature, paintings, movies, and all of the mediums of creativity and imagination and magic.

I'm not quite sure if any of this is actually apparent in my own writing—I don't know if I have reached those sentiments, but I don't know if I ever want to arrive at those emotional destinations because it's the search for them that I love most—to just be an echo of another ghost's dream.

A Catalytic Tilt

So QUIET and awestruck they served witness to sunlit creations, autotrophic sustenance through precipitation and concaved clouds gave way—a path for rays beamed forth from opened beaks, yellow and bright, to let pierce nourished souls sway back to forth. A rocking a stirring a birth among muddied banks—there, there an endothermic hunger to know, to process a breath through leaves and teeth and green-stemmed bark. A starving, beheld—a chemical yield—moon dropped sugar over concentric ridges, soft ripple to stratospheric levels, an epicenter of space. They sucked in and in, until tilted axis tilted over and ocean skies looked upon their journey, their struggle. Photosynthetic they were in need of a palette for the world to spin upon. Chlorophyll, they entwined like famished roots diving. In and up with flared skin, enraged and seeking until finally full to tongue's brim with lifted jaws. And how wearily wearily wearily they haunched as pained bone and thorax. And how they heaved—a strife to dart through rivers in search of warmth to cover their throats and peeled tides to rise over and over and over until exposed organs and vines thrusted themselves toward atomic light, twirling to let the suffocated find solace in blinded manner. To grasp, to cling and climb, to hold with strength and fear, they stood upon fertile soil, not of myths and legends but of love and life—a will to follow welcomed air thresholds. Enter, tipped their way and spread throughout lands with whispered thuds of unknown adventures. Oxygen born from rain and carbon traced back to risen spectacles and heat to shower their spirits for a beginning—upon earth to settle, in vague encounters among strange families, all leaned this way and that.

Yonder Years Ago

So DOWN a synapse they tunneled, carried past sensation burdens: memory waves chute-oscillated, irrigated crevices and canals to harvest minds and remember electric journeys in flashes and sparks. Disconnected and torn, hand-in-hand they went, hesitant and fearful with closed eyes and emptied lungs. They first knew nothing and deemed it better that way. With heavy doubt and trembled silence they asked themselves why embark at all? They whispered these fibers were meant for laceration, were they not? Through molecules and terminals and beyond they went to account their tales of sorrow and sadness. With transmissions and codes, blinks and sighs of moonlit tides and melodies, they jumped from module to module. In gaps of air they briefly forgot and smiled, landed with criss-crossed legs and silenced tongues. Once transmitted came oft-begged times of yonder years, the magnetic pull like rattled chains—each link a glimpse a glance a meander to amnesia. In forests and trails leading to bits of this and that, they felt the stars drop between their fingers, through palms so sleek, there was no grit of sky. And let the constellations fall they did, to a sunrise they recalled when a flock covered darkness momentarily, as they found feather treasures stuck to their mouth roofs. How hollow they felt then, emptied floods of rays on which they encountered infinite love, memories wandered into deep skull pockets, only to be let loose with a storm so polished they gleamed and yearned for more—for more to remember.

Days of Sunlit Marigolds

Tier-caked skies to resemble their minds—a keepsake forever embedded, they tried not to remember days of sunlit marigolds—they knew how it led to sadness. With turned heads—the other way around, clouds below, earth above—their comfort, purgatorial blessings—and so wandered these sways of past worlds of which they no longer sought. Wayward glittered breeze—fresh through, from metallic glimmer of ocean shine, they once thought earth's pole was made of ice—frozen tears built from shadowed sorrows, such a cracked foundation to lean their bodies against. A melting—by time's heat, steady sunset steady sunrise, one by one they go: memories to be forgotten upon rotation. And so all measures and means to let what once was to be gone and sent, they strived to look with opened eyes—easier it was, this way to block all past moons. They questioned themselves—come sun, let enter—leave light, and them, in blinding beams to discover future songs of unknown sensations. Let withered stones mold their minds, shaped and smoothened, plasticity unbound—a rising, a revolution to encompass each and every universal star, a way for them to gather and release all that had been done—to make room for unseen rings and dust. In their eyes they saw refrains drifting toward layered airs, full of need, full of dismay, full of melodic bells in rhythm with all mournings of a solar system—agony and galaxies—to relinquish and escape. So in search they hovered and flailed until legs and arms became still. It was then, when faced with nothing but their own suffering, that was when they found revealed natures of cosmos—that was when they realized a love for the world and its wishes. And so it began.

Skulls of Light

Behold—such sadness, this tilt of candle wick—should it be set to flame, oil and fire, melancholic wax drooped and hung beneath earth. A swayed pendulum, knocking stars upon stars—a musical clink it was, like marbles rattled in their palms. They listened to sorrow as heat won over—bent it became, a sad story of time and sconce and how the labra dipped its way into their skin, settled knop in dirt it thrived to erode its bearing. A bronze of what once was splendor and bold, then only chipped and seared, as if given way to wraths of sky's breath. A meander of such, such that their placated minds irrigated if not eroded into combustion blue and so arrived flickers sounded in gentle furies—their heads turned this way and that to gather shelter in zones of muted memories—ashed vapors to make trails to where they once found meanings of mandibles. Now cracked—cracked smiles, a followed fault line up through braided flames, clavicles of rust and forlorned skulls, hollowed in by melted shapes of their recollections, reflections of amnesiacs—where no longer stories were relayed. Only anesthetic thoughts of fiery creations hovered around—bees of no guidance led them to astrayed crackles and embers. There, they lit their own worlds on fire to find solace in their own burning heads.

Future Memories of Love

SOPORIFIC GLINT—hums of light permeated through their pores, tunneled beams like fresh-born hay and straw wandered upon their craniums to gather and maintain majestic crowns—in circles they hovered to lift themselves forth toward sun's gravity. Tucked between ribs and organs, minerals and stars collected centuries ago from celestial plains—of what once shone in luster then dearth of glaze and sheen—barely a pulse among bones and vines, they strived for reprieve through osmotic tendencies and lended diffusional wraiths. A glimmer: unsheathed flickers of breath, a rattling of thoracic cages—so sternum bent for a crack, clacked and unleashed infinite dust to float toward hydrohelium. So wrapped as they were they heeded luminary songs and tumbled forth, a quench to resolve with solar wishes. Let them live, they whispered into soothed aura, with palmed bits of time they raised their hands to radiate a thirst to fulfill—a message to carry unto those who knew not—they clasped their fingers in hope to remain until their completed task. Let them not be gone just yet, they moved their lips in such a fashion. And so an illumination it was—given by angelic cosmics they left side by side with beating thrill to share a wisdom of past failures. Polished stars and gleam of rib, pebbled minerals and skeletal glow, blinded as they were—in tactile paths they found their ways to account lost histories of love and awe.

Kinetic Electrons

What will it take to mend bones split and scratched and scarred—so they wandered or wondered, whichever they recognized not—small gaps of darkness was all they knew upon rings of Saturn where discs and dust meshed and blended to cause them confusion, a familiar homeostasis. There were marks left on skin for them to remain burdened by star's tenacity—tinged flames upon knuckles and knees, they forgot the meanings of warmth and solace. Solar dirt melded between their teeth—streamed winds blasted upon their faces, they felt the presence of electrons protons particles journeyed from galactic alleys away and how to rest or respond, they looked into each other for slight signals. Temporal endurance—chronos and chime, chromatic spectrums and wavelengths—so such the orbits smiled, causing charged fields to erode their spirits and worn they became. Such were the struggles they mirrored as they tilted their heads to match Saturn's axis to access glimpses of sight and sound and there they met their universe all trapped in patterns across a speckled ocean. Caught in paths of sun's acute vision, angled and veered, angered and leered and oh how quiet the star-filled moss tumbled over, endless glimmered pastures to search for stone and rock, a place to rest and tuck and close their eyes for one last time. Alas, Saturn's belt whirled them to awaken—can they not sleep forever—locked legs, in trance they shuttled and bounced from meteor to meteor, celestial showers to scrub their skin and scalp, a rebirth—a calling—a reckoning, and so no longer trapped but harmonized all in all in time's nurtured embrace.

It Goes Like This

I AM ON the brink of extinction—a strange breeze ventures in, a dizzied morning—a duck here and a duck there, sprinkling sounds of beaks that drift away with the ripples, such ingredients for cinematic echoes. A hush, indeed—so tumbling memories—never a stroll, knock upon the back of my skull, but I find ways to never turn around. Incessant taps—I know that familiar pattering, and I know to lift my tongue only to the knitted skies ahead. Oh, that single cumulus—oh, that drifting boat rocking, as if lost but on it goes into an air so naked, I press my hands against my cloth. If I turn around—so if I turn around, ripped and shredded canvases, left with scars for palettes and splintered brushes, frayed with hollow ghosts, mouths so deep, to enter in meant to never come back, and so angelic are the days to lead me to keep walking, however if I stumble, nonetheless to keep leaning toward the duck here and the duck there—such trumpets to dine my weathered throat. I recognize no one but strangers—I find myself in such strange lands where step upon step lead to more unknowns, knowing that is the entrance into fear, and I've learned to let the fear settle in, to let the fear diffuse through my thoughts because there's no other way. So such strangers—let them be, let them heal, and I listen and I cry, for in the tear of a mother, the voice of a father, a brother's embrace, the palm of a friend, I recognize myself as a stranger who wants to know more about a song that lifts me from staff to staff until I'm just a note waiting to float away toward the soft of a sky, welcoming and blinding, and I fuse myself and let my eyes stay closed for the possibilities are much like the wing of this duck and the wing of that duck, and so I dance on the land of a leaf and let the sun twirl me into a ripple of this pond.

Solar Drifts

So they sawed stars in halves to see the dead inside, and what they saw were remnants of their own beginnings. How should they go about and continue they asked themselves—their palms full of crumbled memories of jubilee, once shining trumpets of soul and glee, now soils of deterioration and whimpered melodies of pain. Shredded stars, stringing through their fingers, lunar rocks and crazed silence bumped and cracked, they scratched their teeth against clumps of moon where they lay in utter loss. Lost were they deemed by their own doing, now such fragile presence—the way light breaks from tumbled skin, they pressed firmly against patted dirt and dust. Their tools, warped and round, decayed teeth and hammer—they chiseled away with the bones of their elbows and knees—to take every star to kill themselves over and over until there was just a glow of sorrow pervading such a sad universe. Beyond the stars they journeyed with weathered voice and eyes, to continue as punishment they gave themselves but wished upon every crater and dune for release and recompense. Dared they to look at each other once it was all done, to face their own mirages amid solar field and stream—they touched hands and felt the sizzle of each other's tips and prints—bellows of weakened throats only traveled as far as their lungs could push. They planted their ankles deep into their barren lands and pulled star after star, gnawing and prying, and dead and dead and dead they found no glimmer or beam. Now on their backs they sought for last breath, for all was too much to fathom—their remnants so deep in chasms of their skulls—there was just a sigh and silence. Let it be gone, they wished. Lo—two shooting stars to defy their wishes—seared through astral skies, against dearth of light, an inertial pulse given a beat, a pattern for them to remember. And like that, oxygenated memories of forthcoming blessings flashed in skull's abyss—an explosion of gleam brought forth redemption and luster—a way they saw to stand again on unknown moons and orbs. Electric and shimmered, they cut these stars of glow with saws anew and sturdy hammer, a tap and a tap—to peer inside to see themselves as one with each other and a nourished future full of marble and twinkled glint.

A Delicate Clef

To WITNESS such calamitous swirls in between glimpses of perceived certitudes—so they thought and so they thought that catastrophic tendencies of nature and order were ways in which they understood. For any other silence in symmetry to cause chaos within systemic procedures, in such gentility and glance, gave way an effect of disturbed notions and sentients. Affected upon stratum and stratum in which they felt battered and however precipitated, pounded and pounded their skulls weathered, over in and over out to where each sight of sun and light they found themselves afloat amid tenuous rope—a rope of vine and illumination to where simple flights of blossomed and torn petals travel up in opposition to gravitational canon. Ripped from ripened soil and stem—with gratitude and vigorous labor, they found an aperture, a song to be held in vibration against earth's palm and throat—altitudes in layers, sheets and swarms, they followed chanted spins of axis and tilt. Hypnotized by consistency of movement and measure, they ventured into endless halls of horizons entwined and weaved into their own lost thorns of existence—braided and clasped as if pined sepal and stamen no longer in search of desire or dirt.

Moon and Mantle

Silt slit—so along the crevice, detritus and echoed lullabies entered and emerged upon river mouths as such tongues lingered among melodic motions up against eroded banks of stalagmitic earth. Lest dearth of photonic strophes to fill air of hallowed matter and grit and to release sediment upon sediment, a bouquet of dirt and mineral in which to rest one's lips as if to kiss gentle vibrations of hum and clef—a world's only ghost, one that sings in soil and sap and how torn it went, the stripped lands and roots. Such is the upheaval of bearings and lost magnets floated in circles around gravitational pulls—pulleys to push belts of tectonic plates and bewildered masses, struck by a touch of love of drained surfaces. This was a way—away each wave however shuddered to find meaning in currents and fields where the radius found its way to a broken beacon, a flickered blink or tap or beat to let simple sheaths of mantle and moon hear in trebles a tumbled soaring sun.

A Lament for My Apparition

When you close your eyes where do I go? I see unfamiliar skin—I recognize your sounds, unknown territories we venture. Where am I to rest? A touch and a touch, to fathom as such is no longer tangible for you and I are simple remains, a reminder of swaying pastures of elongated time. And there is time. Isn't there? We care not for distorted imaginations—I imagine a hunger to be gone and to only be seen when there is no light, just chasms of torment aching for more.

What's in a starved world? But howling throats and swirling stomachs—you and I mean for better thoughts, but you are never gone, are you? Are you here, or do you think I am figments of an existence no longer? Who's to say that I miss you when you're here—who's to say?

I hear your voice in echoes and in echoes your voice wavers until my mind shreds into split memories of you and I or you and you or a song full of tears disappear into a blemished horizon where we are most comforted—that space between your death and my life. Speak—my death and your life.

Speak and let a sun from neither world shine down through my throat so I know you are never there—only here where my bones and blades tremor with love, and your hands hold my head as if it falls from my rusting spine in search of bedrock where we can sleep and no longer wonder who lives and who dies.

Who's to say?

I find you on a torn canvas with spilt acrylic and your eyes float inside my mouth as if marbles in search of a kindred universe where stars knock upon each other for a rhythm to carry on. Your tongue—a tunnel to a land of ash and there's a flicker, a flicker much like when earth tilted in sadness upon a departure. Your arrival, I know not—I hope to never know for you are no ghost and I am dead. Let's say in neither world we meet—either world it is—can there be such a presence such as then when I open my eyes and you are not there I would rather no time for if there's no time there is no you and there is no me—only a mirage of a dream that will never exist, hovering inside a lullaby we never hear.

Come now—a stage with neither entrance or exit, rotating and dizzying. Come now and let me close my eyes one last time—and this time, you won't vanish. Only I dissolve into your home and no longer there is hunger—just a chime to let us know we recognize each other through a breath coming from afar.

m • a

HOWEVER HAUNTED their minds and echoed skulls and tremored bone, they dug for respite and rest—even the frightened sought bark chipped and scratched and highered tiers but they lingered as if any such fear was just a channel to a bay of twilight spark—that which brought a pattern of notes that would lull them for a daze to forget all terrified dreams. But how did they know there was an ending to all time? They knew nothing and perhaps their lacked wisdom gave them more hope in that they never knew how to wish and so they carried on with unknown fervors—heard murmurs of future ghosts, irrigated through their hollowed structures, skeletal and otherwise. They wondered if to scream or shout or cry would rid any domain of unease—these displeased souls, focused and unrelented shuddered to no one, no one at all. Should they close their eyes? Would they return they pondered amid a clash of shrouds machinated and floated above their crowns as hypnotized fables. Mechanical, they argued against natural magnetic pulls, such gravity, and looked around with shut teeth as to block any darkness in pursuit. Wicked ways there were no boundaries or tenets, just an ever flow of no remorse and such vibrated laughter rang and knocked between cartilage and skin—they refused to cover the flanks of their faces for that was all they never knew. How could it be then, through all banter and trembled tongues, that in which such despise and fury to cause an undoing of lives with intentions beyond existence, for them to prevail against such a force of mass and acceleration—atoms only they were but particles together they recognized bonded strength. And with hands shaken and flickered, they held each other to view all that was before them—a melee of all times, brawled and mixed and twirled memories to come and past realities to release—come silence they embraced and surpassed their obstacles with such a love, the world shifted in slight fashion to give attention to such a passion never seen before. And so they walked side by side down tilted earth toward lost beginnings—no more static to mute, enigmatic in wander, yes, and so they walked into discovery.

Harmonic Oscillations

There's a songbird in my head—I can't imagine it but I can hear it, and the melody, a million songs in one, variations and striations creating stairs in my mind, and it never stops and there are a million songs in one—a million songs in one which bursts into a sky, my cranium full of chorus and choir and every now and then I'll open my eyes just in case I'm not a ghost who hasn't flown away, and there's a bird beyond the sun—I sing to it and wonder if it's the one I can't imagine.

Dream Blizzard

When I close my eyes, you fade into the dark—disappear like a famished ghost—I never know if I should open my eyes again to let in the light because either way, there's pain, and hungry for relief from such fashions I remain in your dream or mine, and it's only in this manner, I can exist—in that moment just before you are gone from neither world.

ACKNOWLEDGMENTS

"Upon a Sunny Day at Noon" appeared in *Milk Candy*; "The Learning Game" appeared in *Jellyfish Review*; "Chapel of Ghosts" appeared in *Tiny Molecules*; "Musica Universalis and the Pythagorean Love Song" appeared in *Terse*; "$1000 To Lose" appeared in *mac(ro)mic*; "Like Hummingbirds" appeared in *X-R-A-Y*; "Remember Nothing" appeared in *New Sinews*; "Candles and Petals" appeared in *Bull*; "Rickshaw Wrench and Spoke" appeared in *The Remnant Archive*; "Photospheric Magnifications" appeared in *Crack The Spine*; "Acorns of Memories" appeared in *Truffle Literary Magazine*; "The Sisters" appeared in *Wigleaf*; "A Distance of Thunder," "Such Velocity," "Yonder Years Ago," and "A Catalytic Tilt" appeared in *Fractured*; "Kinetic Electrons," "Future Memories of Love," and "m • a" appeared in *The Art of Everyone*; "A Brief Introduction to Memory" appeared in *Reservoir Road*; "A Delicate Clef," "Fission and Fusion," and "Days of Sunlit Marigolds" appeared in *Flash Boulevard*; "Solar Drifts" appeared in *Nurture*; "Skulls of Light" appeared in *MORIA*; "Her Garden Her Earth" appeared in

Middle House Review; "A Lament for My Apparition" appeared in *Cloves Literary*; "A Slight Tremor" appeared in *Complete Sentence*; "Moon and Mantle" appeared in *Bureau Dispatch*; "Dream Blizzard" appeared in *The Dillydoun Review*; "Signs of Communication" appeared in *Bright Flash*; "A Kolkata Dream" appeared in *New World Writing*; "Listen to Track #10" appeared in *HAD*; "A Vague Recollection from 111 Liberty Avenue" appeared in *Scrawl Place*; "Excerpts from My Memory" appeared in *Schuylkill Valley*; "When Once I Was Gone" appeared in *Semicolon*; "I Want to See the Music of Your Dreams" appeared in *The Doctor T. J. Eckleburg Review*; "Harmonic Oscillations" appeared in *Twin Pies*; "It Goes Like This" appeared in *Ligeia*; "A Sound of Dew" appeared in *Chaotic Merge*; "Golden Fields" appeared in *JMWW*; "I'll Never Know" appeared in *trampset*; "Say Hi" appeared in *Reckon Review*; "In the Shadow of a Bird" appeared in *Janus Literary*; "Elliott Smith 1–8" appeared in *Big Other*.

THANK YOU

Histories of Memories couldn't have been written without the support, love, and care of the following lovely beings:

Thank you to my friends, who without hesitation, have always shown so much kindness and support—your friendship means so much, truly and sincerely.

Thank you, Mike Bourgeois and Andy LeGoullon. Thank you, Chad and Bianca Cosby. Thank you, Karl Schott and Mandy Migues. Thank you, Luke Sonnier. Thank you, Patrick O'Neil. Thank you, Jerome Moroux. Thank you, Katie Culbert. Thank you, Story Frantzen, Abby Langford, and Jacob Camden. Thank you, Amy Barnes. Thank you, Pat Foran. Thank you, James Yates. Thank you, Gabe Olivier. Thank you, Megan Dobyns. Thank you, Rien Fertel. Thank you, Sean Leon. Thank you, Sam Hebert. Thank you, Casie Dodd. Thank you, Jack B. Bedell, Melissa Llanes Brownlee, and Ra'Niqua Lee for your thoughtful and kind words. Many thanks to all of the print and online journals for giving these pieces a chance. Thank you, Lafayette

Barnes & Noble.

Many thanks to the Literary Community who has provided so much encouragement.

Thank you, Belle Point Press—for all of this.

And to my parents, Sarmistha and Subrata Dasgupta, my brother, Deep, and my sister-in-law, Heidi—I love you all so much. Thank you, always, for being there. Love.

Shome Dasgupta's novel *The Seagull and the Urn* was published by HarperCollins India, and it was republished by Hachette/Headline Accent in the UK as *The Sea Singer*. His experimental *i am here And You Are Gone* won the 2010 OW Press Fiction Contest. His books include the novels *The Muu-Antiques* (Malarkey Books), *Tentacles Numbing* (Thirty West), and *Cirrus Stratus* (Spuyten Duyvil), an experimental book of prose, *Spectacles* (Word West), and a poetry collection, *Iron Oxide* (Assure Press). His writing has appeared in *McSweeney's Internet Tendency*, *Jabberwock Review*, *New Orleans Review*, *New Delta Review*, *American Book Review*, *Arkansas Review*, *Magma Poetry*, and elsewhere. His fiction and poetry have also been anthologized in *Best Small Fictions*, *The &Now Awards 2: The Best Innovative Writing*, and *Poetic Voices Without Borders 2*. His work has been featured as a *storySouth* Million Writers Award Notable Story, and his stories and poems have been nominated for the Pushcart Prize, Best Small Fictions, Best of the Net, Best Microfiction, and the *Orison Anthology*. He lives in Lafayette, Louisiana, and can be found online at shomedome.com and @laughingyeti.

Histories of Memories
was designed, edited, and typeset by
Belle Point Press in Fort Smith, Arkansas.
The text is set in Garamond Premier Pro.

The mission of Belle Point Press is to celebrate the
literary culture and community
of the American Mid-South:
all its paradoxes and contradictions,
all the ways it gets us home.
Visit us at
www.bellepointpress.com.

Fort Smith, Arkansas

www.ingramcontent.com/pod-product-compliance
Lightning Source LLC
LaVergne TN
LVHW091008080826
845145LV00003B/1180

* 9 7 8 1 9 6 0 2 1 5 0 8 6 *